Good Night, Firefly

Gabriel Alborozo

Henry Holt and Company

New York

Special thanks to Kirsten Hall and Sally Doherty,
who let the firefly out of his jar.

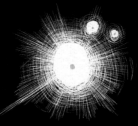

Henry Holt and Company, LLC
Publishers since 1866
175 Fifth Avenue
New York, New York 10010
mackids.com

Library of Congress Cataloging-in-Publication Data
Alborozo, 1972– author, illustrator.
Good night, firefly / Gabriel Alborozo. — First edition.
    pages   cm
Summary: When the power goes off one night, Nina conquers her fear of the dark by
going out and trapping one of the fireflies lighting up the sky, and she has fun playing
with him until she realizes his light is growing ever dimmer and she must set him free.
ISBN 978-1-62779-222-6 (hardback)
[1. Fear of the dark—Fiction. 2. Fireflies—Fiction. 3. Bedtime—Fiction.]
PZ7.1.A43Goo 2015   [E]—dc23   2014037919

Henry Holt books may be purchased for business or promotional use. For information on
bulk purchases, please contact the Macmillan Corporate and Premium Sales Department
at (800) 221-7945 x5442 or by e-mail at specialmarkets@macmillan.com.

First Edition—2015 / Designed by April Ward
The illustrations for this book were created with pen and ink and watercolor, enhanced digitally.
Printed in China by South China Printing Co. Ltd., Dongguan City, Guangdong Province

1 3 5 7 9 10 8 6 4 2

For Katia, my firefly,
and for everyone with a night-light

Nina was scared of the dark,
so it was good she had a night-light,
which made things better.

Then one night . . .

the
electricity
went out.

Nina watched as
scary shadows crept
across her walls.
Every noise sounded like
the whispering of monsters.

"Mom?

Dad?"

They must be fast asleep!
Nina went back to her room.

Through her window, Nina saw a soft yellow glow.
The yard was full of tiny, dancing points of light.

FIREFLIES!

Nina ran outside.
The fireflies whirled and
flashed as Nina lifted her
jar. "Come on, little guy.
Come with me."

Back in her room, the little firefly's
light scared away the shadows.
The only sound was the gentle night breeze.

But there was still one problem.
Nina wasn't sleepy anymore.
What could she do?

She had another idea!

Nina gathered her dolls together
and put out her tea set.
"More tea, Firefly?" she asked.

The firefly's light slowly flicked on
and off. She guessed that meant no.

"Want to make shadow puppets, Firefly?" she asked.

Nina held her hands up into his light. First she made a rabbit.

Then a duck
and a dinosaur.

But the firefly blinked
slower and slower.
And the shadow
animals grew dimmer.

Nina was about to play dress-up when
she noticed how dark it was getting.

Peering into his jar, she saw
the firefly lying at the bottom.
His light had become very faint.

Nina tried everything she could think of
to make his light stronger—

a battery,

a wind-up key,

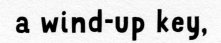

her favorite
chocolate bar—

but nothing
worked.

Under the tree, a sparkle of
fireflies blinked and swirled
as she turned the lid.

Her little firefly slowly rose up
and out of the jar. As he flew
higher and higher, his light
became brighter and brighter.

Back in bed, Nina gazed
at the soft light glowing
through her window.

"Good night, Firefly," she whispered.